THE GHOST ZONE

Jokes, Riddles, Tongue Twisters & "Daffynitions"

By Gary Chmielewski

Illustrated by Jim Caputo

Read Jokes. Write Jokes.

Ha! Ha! Ha! Ha! Ha! Ha! Ha! Ha! Ha! Ha! Ha! Ha!

NORWOOD HOUSE PRESS

A Note to Parents and Caregivers:

As the old saying goes, "Laughter is the best medicine." It's true for reading as well. Kids naturally love humor, so why not look to their interests to get them motivated to read? The Funny Zone series features books that include jokes, riddles, word plays, and tongue twisters—all of which are sure to delight your young reader.

We invite you to share this book with your child, taking turns to read aloud to one another, practicing timing, emphasis, and expression. You and your child can deliver the jokes in a natural voice, or have fun creating character voices and exaggerating funny words. Be sure to pause often to make sure your child understands the jokes. Talk about what you are reading and use this opportunity to explore new vocabulary words and ideas. Reading aloud can help your child build confidence in reading.

Along with being fun and motivating, humorous text involves higher order thinking skills that support comprehension. Jokes, riddles, and word plays require us to explore the creative use of language, develop word and sound recognition, and expand vocabulary.

At the end of the book there are activities to help your child develop writing skills. These activities tap your child's creativity by exploring numerous types of humor. Children who write materials based on the activities are encouraged to send them to Norwood House Press for publication on our website or in future books. Please see page 24 for details.

Above all, the most important part of the reading experience is to have fun and enjoy it!

Sincerely,

Shannon Cannon

Shannon Cannon
Literacy Consultant

NORWOOD HOUSE PRESS

P.O. Box 316598 • Chicago, Illinois 60631
For information regarding Norwood House Press, please visit our website at:
www.norwoodhousepress.com or call 866-565-2900.

Editor: Jessy McCulloch
Designer: Design Lab

Library of Congress Cataloging-in-Publication Data:
Chmielewski, Gary, 1946–
  The ghost zone / by Gary Chmielewski ; illustrated by Jim Caputo.
    p. cm. — (The funny zone)
  Summary: "Book contains 100 ghost-themed jokes, tongue twisters and "Daffynitions". Backmatter includes creative writing information and exercises. After completing the exercises, the reader is encouraged to write their own jokes and submit them for web site posting and future Funny Zone editions. Full-color illustrations throughout"—Provided by publisher.
  ISBN-13: 978-1-59953-297-4 (library edition : alk. paper)
  ISBN-10: 1-59953-297-2 (library edition : alk. paper) 1.
Ghosts—Juvenile humor. I. Caputo, Jim. II. Title.
  PN6231.G45C46 2009
  818'.5402—dc22   2008033635

Manufactured in the United States of America in North Mankato, Minnesota   163R-052010

BOO!

What type of mistakes do ghosts make?
Boo-boos!

What kind of snakes do ghosts fear the most?
Boo-a constrictors!

What do you call a ghost with a broken leg?
Hoblin' Goblin!

Why did the ghost sing off-key?
He left his sheet music at home!

What do near-sighted ghosts wear?
Spooktacles!

Where do ghosts buy their sheets?
At store 'white sales'!

Why did the ghost cross the road?
To get to 'The Other Side'.

What happens when a ghost is lost in the fog?
He is *mist*!

How can you tell if a ghost is about to faint?
He gets as pale as a sheet!

What college do ghosts usually graduate from?
Boo-kley!

Why does a ghost get upset when it rains?
The rain dampens its spirits!

What should you do when a ghost can't understand what you say?
Spook a little slower!

Why are ghosts such bad magicians?
Their tricks are so revealing!

What is a ghost-proof cycle?
One with no spooks in it!

What should you do with overweight ghosts?
Exorcise them!

Did the ghoul give you good directions to the cemetery?
Yes, they were dead on!

What is the best way to get rid of a demon?
Exorcise regularly!

Why are ghosts bad at telling lies?
You can see right through them!

How do you begin a ghost story?
"Once upon a tomb …"

Why don't ghouls get up before sunrise?
It never dawned on them!

Why is it good to tell ghost stories in hot weather?
They are so chilling!

GOING HAUNTING

What kind of TV do you find in a haunted house?
A big scream!

When do ghosts usually appear?
Just before someone screams!

Knock, Knock.
Who's there?
Ghost.
Ghost who?
Ghost slowly when you walk through a haunted house.

Where do you find a missing ghost?
At his favorite haunt!

What happens when a ghost haunts a theater?
The actors get stage fright!

Why did the car stop when it saw a ghost?
It had a nervous breakdown!

What is the one room in a house that ghosts avoid?
The living room!

Why did the game warden arrest the ghost?
He didn't have a *haunting* license!

What is a ghost's favorite song?
"A-Haunting We Will Go ..."

What happened when the tree saw the ghost?
It was petrified!

What ghost haunted the King of England in the 18th century?
"The Spirit of '76!"

When do ghosts haunt skyscrapers?
When they are in high spirits!

Were the neighbors able to sell their haunted houses?
Nope, they didn't stand a ghost of a chance.

Why did the ghost starch her scarf?
She wanted everyone to be scared stiff!

Where do ghosts live?
In their *terrortory*!

What do you call a ghost in a torn sheet?
A holy terror!

Why was the ghost afraid?
It was spooked!

What would you get if you crossed a ghost with a pair of trousers?
A scaredy pants!

What's a ghost's motto?
"Scare and scare alike!"

Why are graveyards noisy?
Because of all the *coffin*!

Javier: "I'll stop being frightened if you'll stop being scared."
Tannia: "That sounds like a fear trade to me."

9

GHOSTLY GOODIES

What do you call a demon who slurps his food?
A goblin!

What do ghosts serve for dessert?
Ice scream!

What do ghosts add to their morning cereal?
Booberries!

What do little ghosts drink?
Evaporated milk!

Where do ghosts buy their food?
At the ghostery store!

What kind of candy do ghosts and goblins never eat?
Life Savers!

What does a ghost eat for lunch?
A Boo-logna sandwich!

Knock, Knock.
Who's there?
Goblin.
Goblin who?
Goblin all your food up at once will
only give you a tummy ache.

11

WORKING STIFFS

How did the glamorous ghoul earn a living?
She was a cover ghoul!

VANITY SCARE

Ghoulia
Roberts

Doom
and
Gloomy
Rooms

Our Grossly &
Mostly Ghostly
Restaurants

SPECIAL ISSUE

Who speaks at a ghost's press conference?
The spooksperson.

What is a devil's picket line called?
A **demon**stration!

Where do you find the names of famous ghosts?
In "Boo's Who"!

Who wrote the recent best-seller about haunted houses?
A ghostwriter of course!

Where do old spirits move when they retire?
To a ghost town!

What do you call the ghost of a door-to-door salesperson?
A dead ringer!

What branch of the military service do ghouls serve in?
The Ghost Guard!

What did the ghost teacher say to her class?
Just watch the board and I'll go through it again!

What happened when the ghosts went on strike?
A skeleton staff took over!

LOVE GHOST

Why aren't ghosts very popular dates?
They aren't much to look at!

**How do ghosts break up
with their ghoulfriends?**
They just disappear!

Why do ghouls and demons hang out together?
Demons are a ghoul's best friend!

Tina wanted to marry a ghost.
I don't know what possessed her!

What does a good-looking ghost look like?
He is very hauntsome!

What do you call a ghost and a zombie that go out on a date?
Boo-friend and ghoul-friend!

BIG GHOSTS, SMALL GHOSTS

Where do baby ghosts go during the day?
To the dayscare center!

JR.
Jeepers
Creepers

What did the mother ghost say to the baby ghost?
"Be sure to put your boos and shocks on!"

What did the mother ghost say to the baby ghost?

"Fasten your sheet belt!"

What do baby ghosts wear on their feet?
Bootees!

What did the mommy ghost say to the baby ghost?
"Don't spook until you're spooken to!"

What do you call a ghost's mother and father?

Transparents!

What do you call a ghost born just after World War II?
A baby boooomer!

What are little ghosts dressed in when it rains?
Bootees and ghouloshes!

How do ghosts get to school in the morning?
They take the ghoul bus!

GHOSTLY FUN

What do demons have on vacation?
A devil of a time!

Why do ghosts give dull parties?
No one is ever the 'life of the party'!

What nursery rhyme do ghosts like read to them?
Little Boo Peep!

What is a ghost's favorite party game?
Hide-and-go-shriek!

What do little ghosts like more than a frisbee?
Boomerangs!

What type of tie does a ghost like to wear to a formal party?
A boo-tie!

What game do ghosts like to play?
Peek-a-**Boo**!

What kind of songs do ghosts like?
Haunting melodies!

What is a ghost's favorite article of clothing?
Boo jeans!

What type of music do ghosts prefer?
Spirituals, of course!

Who is a ghost's favorite nursery rhyme character?
Little Boy Boo!

What is a ghost's favorite color?

Light boo!

What mail do ghosts like to send?

Chain letters!

Mas-scare-a!

What is a ghost's favorite day of the week?
Frightday!

Did you hear about the ghoul's favorite hotel?
It had running rot and mold!

What is a ghost's favorite position?
Horror-zontal!

What do ghosts say when something is really great?
"Ghoul!"

What race do ghosts love to watch?
A scareathon!

Why do ghosts make great cheerleaders?
They have lots of spirit!

MAKING STORIES OUT OF YOUR JOKES!

Most ghost stories are meant to be scary. But sometimes the best ghost stories are funny, too. Put the two together and you give new meaning to the phrase "scared silly."

Whatever kind of ghost story is your favorite, there's no denying how much fun they are to tell and hear. And the best way to keep the ghost story tradition alive is to write some of your own.

YOU TRY IT!

The hardest part about writing your own stories is deciding where to start. That doesn't have to be a problem though, because you can use some of these jokes to write your very own ghost stories!

It is important to begin with a plan about the kind of story you want to tell. For example from page 4:

What happens when a ghost is lost in the fog?
He is *mist*!

From this joke, you could write a story about a ghost that gets separated from his family and friends on a foggy day. By the time the fog fades, he has no idea where he is or how to get back home. This is where it gets fun, because you can let your imagination take over.

What kinds of different places does the ghost go? What kinds of things does he see? Who does he meet along the way? What does he learn during his journey to return home?

You can make your story as long or as short as you want. You can also decide how scary or funny to make it. Then on the next dark and stormy night, you can impress your family and friends with a ghost story they haven't heard before!

SEND US YOUR JOKES!

Pick out the best scary story that you created and send it to us at Norwood House Press. We will publish it on our website — organized according to grade level, the state you live in, and your first name.

Selected jokes might also appear in a future special edition book, *Kids Write in the Funny Zone*. If your joke is included in the book, you and your school will receive a free copy.

Here's how to send the jokes to Norwood House Press:
1) Go to www.norwoodhousepress.com.
2) Click on the **Enter the Funny Zone** tab.
3) Select and print the joke submission form.
4) Fill out the form, include your joke, and send to:
> The Funny Zone
> Norwood House Press
> PO Box 316598
> Chicago, IL 60631

Here's how to see your joke posted on the website:
1) Go to www.norwoodhousepress.com.
2) Click on the **Enter the Funny Zone** tab.
3) Select **Kids Write in the Funny Zone** tab.
4) Locate your grade level, then state, then first name.
> If it's not there yet check back again.